DINK, JOSH, AND RUTH ROSE AREN'T THE
ONLY KID DETECTIVES!

WHAT ABOUT YOU?

CAN YOU FIND THE HIDDEN MESSAGE
INSIDE THIS BOOK?

There are 26 illustrations in this book, not counting the one on the title page, the map at the beginning, and the picture of the space shuttle that repeats at the start of many of the chapters. In each of the 26 illustrations, there's a hidden letter. If you can find all the letters, you will spell out a secret message!

If you're stumped, the answer is on the bottom of page 133.

HAPPY DETECTING!

This book is dedicated to reading kids and reading parents.
—R.R.

To Payton and Abigail
—J.S.G.

Text copyright © 2020 by Ron Roy
Cover art copyright © 2020 by Stephen Gilpin
Interior illustrations copyright © 2020 by John Steven Gurney

Many thanks to Viki Ash of the San Antonio Public Library for compiling the list of titles for further reading on pages 135–136.

Visit us on the Web!
rhcbooks.com

Educators and librarians, for a variety of teaching tools,
visit us at RHTeachersLibrarians.com

Library of Congress Cataloging-in-Publication Data
Names: Roy, Ron, author. | Gurney, John Steven, illustrator.
Title: Space shuttle scam / by Ron Roy; illustrated by John Steven Gurney.
Description: New York: Random House, [2020] | Series: A to Z mysteries.
Super edition; 12 | "A Stepping stone book." |
Summary: Dink, Josh, and Ruth Rose head to Florida, where they uncover a scam at a local space memorabilia attraction. | Includes bibliographical references.
Identifiers: LCCN 2019019070 | ISBN 978-0-525-57889-5 (trade) |
ISBN 978-0-525-57890-1 (lib. bdg.) | ISBN 978-0-525-57891-8 (ebook)
Subjects: | CYAC: Swindlers and swindling—Fiction. | Florida—Fiction. |
Mystery and detective stories.
Classification: LCC PZ7.R8139 Sn 2020 | DDC [Fic]—dc23

Printed in the United States of America
10 9 8 7 6 5 4 3

A to Z Mysteries®

SUPER EDITION 12

Space Shuttle Scam

by Ron Roy

illustrated by
John Steven Gurney

A STEPPING STONE BOOK™

Random House 🏠 New York

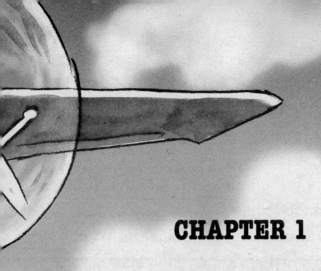

CHAPTER 1

Walker Wallace turned the engine key and adjusted the throttle. The propeller began whirring as he let up on the foot brakes. His small airplane raced down the airport runway in Hartford, Connecticut, then lifted into the April sky. "We're off!" he cried.

Dink, Josh, and Ruth Rose were buckled into the seats behind Walker. Walker's sister Wallis sat in the front passenger seat. "Florida, here we come!" she said.

"Am I going to get airsick?" Josh asked.

"You'd better not," Dink said. "I'm right next to you!"

"Me too," said Ruth Rose, who sat on Josh's other side.

The kids wore jeans and sweatshirts. Ruth Rose liked to have everything match, so her headband, shirt, and jeans were the color of spring violets. Her sneakers and backpack were the same color.

"We should have a smooth ride," Wallis said. "We'll be in Florida before you know it!"

Wallis Wallace was the kids' favorite mystery book writer, and their friend. She was going to Florida to visit her aunt Alice, and had invited Dink, Josh, and Ruth Rose to join her. They were headed for the town of Christmas, Florida, where Aunt Alice lived. She ran Alice's Space Shuttle, a small museum where kids could see space stuff up close.

"How's Abbi?" Ruth Rose asked Wallis.

Abigail, who liked being called Abbi,

was Wallis's adopted daughter. She was born with spina bifida, so she used a wheelchair to get around.

"Fine, thanks," Wallis said. "This week, she's at camp, and she's learning to ride a horse!"

"Can you tell us what your new book is about?" Dink asked Wallis.

"I only have part of the story worked out," Wallis said, turning to look at the kids. "It's about an astronaut who accidentally leaves his cat on the moon after a mission." She grinned. "The cat's name is Blinky, and I have to figure out how to get him back to Earth!"

"Can't the astronaut just return to the moon and get Blinky?" Dink asked.

Wallis shook her head. "Moon launches are super expensive," she said. "And the missions use a lot of fuel, so it would cost millions of dollars to go back to the moon. Until I come up with an idea, the cat is stuck up there!"

"Poor Blinky!" Ruth Rose said. "He'll be so lonely!"

"And hungry!" Josh said.

The small plane sailed higher. The kids gazed through the windows at the clouds. Dink wondered if there were clouds over the moon. He decided he'd look it up later. His laptop was tucked inside his backpack.

Ruth Rose was flipping the pages of her guidebook. "Wow, a lot of wild animals live in Florida," she said. "Want me to read the list?"

"No, thanks," Josh muttered.

"Please tell us!" Dink said. He and Ruth Rose liked to tease Josh. They knew he wasn't a fan of wild animals.

Ruth Rose opened the book and read: "Florida Flora and Fauna."

"What are flora and fauna?" Josh asked.

"*Flora* means plants, and *fauna* means animals," Dink said.

"How do you know that?" Josh asked.

Dink tapped the side of his head. "Dink brain," he said.

Josh laughed. "Okay," he said to Ruth Rose. "What animals live in Florida?"

"Lots of stuff," Ruth Rose said. "Pumas, bears, snakes, alligators—"

"Yikes! Stop the plane! I want to get off!" Josh yelled.

"Plus mosquitoes, butterflies, raccoons, eagles, frogs, fish, turtles, lizards, and spiders," Ruth Rose continued.

"You forgot to mention the Red Gobbler," Dink said.

Josh closed his eyes. "What's a Red Gobbler?" he asked.

Dink just grinned.

"How about a hint, Clint?" Josh asked, trying not to grin.

"Well, they have red hair," Dink said. "And they gobble!"

The plane's loud humming and the vibration coming through his seat made Dink feel drowsy. He closed his eyes.

"Wakey-wakey," Wallis said. She reached around and tapped Dink on the knee. "We're almost there. Walker is going to fly us over Aunt Alice's house before we land at the airport."

Dink sat up, rubbed his eyes, and peered through his window. He saw more clouds.

"Right now, we're over Kennedy Space Center," Walker said over his shoulder. "Sorry about the clouds."

A few minutes later, the kids looked

down on a small town. Buildings and cars looked like pieces in a board game.

Walker took his plane lower. "Any minute now . . . there! See that white house? That's where Aunt Alice lives!"

The kids looked down and saw a house and barn. Spreading wide behind the barn was a jungle-like forest that seemed to go on for miles. Two cars were parked in the driveway on the right side of the house.

"We'll land in about five minutes," Walker said. He turned the plane and headed for the airport.

CHAPTER 2

"There's the airport," Walker said.

The kids looked down and saw parked planes, buildings with flat roofs, and a parking lot. SPACE COAST REGIONAL AIRPORT was painted in huge letters on a roof.

Walker landed the plane and taxied to one of the buildings. "Welcome to Christmas, Florida," he said.

Walker and Wallis helped the kids deplane. They collected their backpacks and walked toward the building.

"It's hotter here than in Connecticut!" Josh said.

"Well, it gets warmer," Wallis said.

"Be thankful this is April and not July!"

She looked toward the parking area. "Aunt Alice is usually here to meet us," she said. "But we saw her station wagon in the driveway."

"Let's give her a few minutes," Walker said. "Maybe she just forgot. . . ."

"Walker, you know Aunt Alice never forgets anything!" his sister said.

Dink looked around the airport. He saw tall palm trees and short buildings. One bird flew over. Everything was hot and quiet.

"Finally!" Wallis said. She waved at a station wagon that was heading toward them.

The station wagon Dink had seen parked by the white house pulled up and stopped. A young guy with blond hair in a ponytail hopped out and waved. "Hi, I'm Kenny," he said. "I work for Ms. Wallace. She asked me to come get you."

Kenny wore baggy shorts, a tank top,

and flip-flops. His skin was tanned deep brown. A tiny glass earring sparkled from his left earlobe.

"Sorry I'm late," Kenny said. "I had to bring something to my uncle at the bank where he works."

"Hi, Kenny," Walker said. The men shook hands. "I'm Walker. This is my sister Wallis, and these are our friends Dink, Josh, and Ruth Rose."

"Nice to meet y'all," Kenny said.

Walker hugged his sister. "I'll see you tomorrow," he said. "Some of my pals work at Kennedy Space Center and are getting together tonight, and I told them I'd join them. You're still planning to make Aunt Alice a birthday cake tomorrow, right?"

Wallis nodded. "Don't be late!" she said.

The kids thanked Walker, and he trotted back to his plane.

"Where's my aunt?" Wallis asked Kenny. "I thought she'd be picking us up."

Kenny put the luggage in the back of the station wagon. "Um, she was going to, but she's pretty upset," he said.

"What is she upset about?" Wallis asked.

"I'll tell you on the way," Kenny said.

They piled into the station wagon. Kenny drove out of the airport parking lot and turned left.

Wallis looked at Kenny. "You were saying . . . ?" she asked.

"A mountain lion was hanging around your aunt's house this morning," Kenny said.

"Oh no!" Wallis said.

"Ms. Wallace was inside," Kenny went on. "The lion was in the driveway, just watching the house. Maybe it smelled her dog. I managed to get a picture on my phone before it ran away."

Dink, Josh, and Ruth Rose were listening to every word. "Did the mountain lion escape from a zoo?" Josh asked.

Wallis turned around to face the kids. "There *are* mountain lions in the wild in Florida," she said, smiling a little. "They're also known as cougars or pumas. We almost never see them because they stay away from people."

No one spoke for the next few miles. "How long are y'all staying with Ms. Wallace?" Kenny asked.

"Just the weekend," Wallis said. "So you work for my aunt? I didn't know she'd hired anyone."

"I started in January," Kenny said. "Just part-time. I go to the community college here in Christmas."

"That was just after my uncle died," Wallis said. "And what do you do for Aunt Alice?"

"I help out when teachers bring their classes to see the space barn," Kenny said. "I also run the café, and I help Howie if he needs me."

"Who's Howie?" Wallis asked.

"He works for your aunt, too," Kenny said. "He mows the lawn and keeps the place looking good. Howie's a handy dude."

"Well, I'm glad she has you both," Wallis said.

"Oh, and there's Hanna," Kenny said. "She comes a couple times a week to help your aunt around the house. When kids visit, Hanna shows them around the barn."

"What's in the barn?" Josh asked.

Wallis turned and grinned. "That's where my uncle kept all his space stuff," she said. "You'll see it soon."

Dink poked Josh on the arm and pointed out the window. Nailed to a post was a sign that said SNAKE WORLD! Y'ALL COME ON IN!

Josh closed his eyes and shook his head.

A few minutes later, Kenny turned the car into the gravel driveway. They passed under a wooden replica of a space shuttle. The silver shuttle was about fifteen feet long and hung on chains from trees on both sides of the driveway.

"That is so cool!" Josh said.

"The space shuttle is new," Wallis

said. "I haven't seen it before."

"Howie painted it," Kenny said. He parked the station wagon behind a gray van.

Wallis and the kids hopped out and got their luggage. Kenny scuffed his foot in the gravel. "Right here's where the mountain lion was," he said. "The thing's tail was almost touching this car!"

Everyone looked at the spot. Dink gulped. The animal had been only ten feet from the house!

"The place looks great!" Wallis said. The house was white with black shutters. The windows gleamed in the sunlight, over window boxes planted with a variety of flowers.

A tall man carrying a ladder strode across the yard toward them. He wore jeans, a blue T-shirt, and thick-soled work boots. "Hi there," the man said. "I'm Howard Booker, but you can call me Howie."

He laid the ladder down on the lawn and stuck out a big hand to shake. When Dink shook, his own hand seemed to disappear.

"You're here!" a voice cried. A plump woman with white hair and eyeglasses came through a side door.

Wallis and her aunt hugged, and then the kids stepped forward to greet her. Dink put out his hand, but Alice pulled him into a hug. "We're big huggers here in the South!" she said.

After she'd hugged Josh and Ruth Rose, Alice brought them inside to the kitchen. On the table, Dink noticed a bag of flour, a mixing bowl, a jug of milk, and a pan with a dozen spoonfuls of cookie dough.

"Wallis told me you kids like cookies," Alice said.

Josh started to say something about how *much* he liked cookies. But he stopped when something licked his hand.

CHAPTER 3

Josh pulled his hand away and let out a yelp. A small bundle of fur with shining black eyes was looking up at him.

"This is my sweet dog, Bear," Alice said. "He's just saying hello to you, Josh. But he *is* hungry for these cookies I'm about to pop in the oven."

Alice opened the kitchen door. "Outside, little Bear," she ordered. "Go help Howie clean the gutters!" The dog hopped across the threshold and took off around a corner of the house.

"Bear adores Howie," she said. "You should see this place when Howie brings his kids over. They chase Bear, and he chases them right back!"

She started wiping the table. "Dink, be a dear and put the milk in the fridge, would you?"

Dink opened the fridge and slid the milk jug inside. He noticed a bunch of magnets sticking to the fridge door. One was a plastic alligator, holding a note in its mouth. In big handwriting, the note said:

PLEASE BUY MORE PAPER TOWELS. H.

"Aunt Alice, Kenny told us about the mountain lion this morning," Wallis said. "You must have been terrified!"

"I didn't see the critter, but poor Kenny was pretty shook," she said. "I was in the house. Suddenly he came running in the back door and showed me a picture of the lion on his cell phone. I ran to the window, but by then it was gone."

"Well, I'm glad nothing worse happened," Wallis said.

"It's not the mountain lion I'm worried about," Alice said. "Kenny said he'd seen alligators and snakes by the pond out back." Alice shuddered. "Now, snakes and gators I can do without, especially with little Bear playing in the yard!"

Just then, they all heard a small engine. Dink looked through the kitchen door and saw a thin woman with red hair climb off a motor scooter. She was wearing shorts, a T-shirt, and sandals.

"That'll be Hanna," Alice said.

The woman came into the kitchen, carrying some mail, and Alice introduced everyone. "My niece and her friends came all the way from Connecticut to see me," Alice said.

"Pleased to meet you," Hanna said. "I'll make y'all some lemonade." She left the mail on the table and walked into the pantry.

"That'll be lovely, hon," Alice said as she looked through her mail. "My husband liked the articles in this." She slid a magazine called *Super Science* over to Dink.

The magazine cover showed two guys in rubber boots wading in a green pond. The caption read GREEN GOO THAT CAN SAVE THE PLANET!

Alice picked up a white card that was mixed among her envelopes. "Oh drat, here's another of these dumb postcards!" she said.

"What postcards, Auntie?" Wallis asked.

"Someone wants to buy this house and property," Alice said. "They keep pestering me. I've gotten half a dozen postcards in the past few weeks."

She slid it over to Wallis, who read it aloud:

IF YOU ARE INTERESTED IN SELLING YOUR HOME, PLEASE CALL OR TEXT ME IMMEDIATELY!
321-555-9000. SINCERELY, M.K.

Wallis said, "Your address is on it, but there's no stamp."

"I guess they just stick the postcards in my mailbox," Alice said.

"It's signed *M.K.*," Wallis said. "Who's that?"

Her aunt shrugged. "No idea," she said, dropping the postcard into a drawer near the fridge. "I haven't gotten back to the person. Then, a week ago, a woman started calling. Don't know how she got my number, but she said she wanted to buy my house. Said she'd pay cash! Good thing Hanna took the calls, or I would've told her something not very nice!"

"Are you thinking of selling?" Wallis asked.

Alice shook her head, then sighed. "Maybe I should," she said. "Just get a small, safe apartment in town. No animals, no burglars. But, darn it, I don't *want* to move!"

"Burglars!" Wallis said. She took her aunt's hand. "Auntie, have you been *robbed*?"

"Not the house," Alice said. "A few weeks ago, I noticed that your uncle's diary and his favorite fountain pen had gone missing from his desk in the barn. His father gave him that pen, and Barney treasured it. Oh, and a batch of letters he saved in a file folder are also gone."

"Are you sure the things were stolen?" Wallis asked. "Could Uncle Barney have put them away someplace?"

"Hanna and I searched the desk and the barn," Alice said. "Those things were there a few weeks ago, and then—poof!—they were gone. Maybe I have ghosts in my barn!"

Josh gulped loudly.

"Don't mind me, young man!" Alice said. "I'm just fretting. Now, come see where you're sleeping."

"And I'm going upstairs for a shower and a nap!" Wallis told her aunt.

Alice slid a tray of cookies into the oven. "You kids follow me!"

"I'll bring the lemonade," Hanna said.

"Lovely, hon," Alice said. She grabbed a key ring from a hook by the door and herded Dink, Josh, and Ruth Rose out to the yard.

"Aren't we sleeping in the house?" Dink asked.

Alice shook her head. "I have a special place just for kids!" she said. "Follow me."

Alice took them down a stone path across the lawn. Dink noticed a picnic table in the shade of some oak trees. A tall red barn stood at the end of the path, and Dink could see a pond behind it.

Long sheets of feathery-looking gray stuff hung from the oak tree branches. "What's that stuff?" Josh asked. He stood on tiptoes and tried to reach some that hung over his head.

"Spanish moss," Alice said. "My husband used to call it *Grandpa's beard*. I wouldn't touch it, though. All kinds of critters live inside it!"

"What kind of critters?" Josh asked, pulling his hand back.

"It's a favorite place for mosquitoes to hide," Alice said. "Spiders go in to eat the mosquitoes. Bats fly in to eat the spiders, and snakes climb up there to eat the bats!"

Josh looked down at the ground. "Are there a lot of snakes around here?" he asked.

Alice nodded. "Plenty of snakes live in Florida, but only a few types are venomous," she said, walking toward the barn.

"What's *VEN-uh-mus*?" Josh whispered.

"It means *poisonous*," Ruth Rose said.

CHAPTER 4

The barn door was secured with a pad-lock. The sliding door was decorated with a painting of a space shuttle hur-tling across a blue sky. A sign above the door said WELCOME TO THE SPACE SHUTTLE.

"Howie painted this door and sign last week," Alice said. "Isn't it wonderful?"

"He's really good," Josh said.

To the right of the door, a small room had been added to the barn. Dink saw a sign that said COMET CAFÉ. There were a few tables and chairs in front, sitting in the shade of a tall palm tree.

"Teachers bring classes of kids to see

the barn," Alice said. "No kids are coming this week because of spring vacation, but when schools are in session, I get a couple of busloads a week."

On the left side of the sliding door, another room jutted out from the barn wall. The room had four windows and a bright yellow screen door.

"This is the bunkhouse, where you'll sleep," Alice said. She pushed the screen door open, making the hinges creak like a door in a scary movie.

Alice flipped on a light switch. The walls were light purple, like the sky just before it gets dark. A mobile of the planets and the sun hung from the ceiling. Bunk beds stood against opposite walls. Dink noticed a bathroom at the end of the room.

"This is excellent!" Josh said. "Who made the cool mobile?"

"Howie, and he did all the painting, too," Alice said. "When horses lived in

the barn, the saddles and food were kept here. My husband and Howie added a bathroom and built the bunks."

Josh leaned toward Ruth Rose's ear. "The walls almost match your outfit," he said with a grin. "Like a blueberry milkshake."

"My outfit is the color of spring flowers," Ruth Rose told Josh.

Dink looked through one of the window screens. "Why is the pond all green?" he asked.

"That's algae," Alice said. "Green slimy stuff that grows like crazy here. My husband asked some scientists about it, and they told him algae grows so fast because of the fertilizer people use on their lawns."

"This bunkhouse is perfect," Ruth Rose said. "Thanks a lot, Auntie A."

"You're entirely welcome," Alice answered. "Pick your beds, but check the blankets for scorpions."

"You're kidding, right?" Josh asked.

"We have three kinds of scorpions in Florida," Alice said. "None of them are deadly, but they have a nasty sting!"

She pulled a purple blanket off one of the lower bunks and shook it out. Then she ran her hand inside the pillowcase and sheets. "Nothing hiding in there," she said.

Josh threw his backpack on the bed Alice had just checked.

"Oh, and peek inside your shoes

before you put 'em on in the morning," Alice said. "Scorpions like to hide in dark places."

"No way!" Josh said. "I'm sleeping with my sneakers on!"

Dink tossed his backpack on the bunk above Josh's. "I won't let any critters get you, Josh," he said.

Josh shook his head. "We don't have scorpions in Connecticut!" he mumbled.

"I'll leave you to get settled," Alice said. "Come for lemonade when—"

Suddenly a scream came through the windows.

"WHAT ON EARTH!" Alice cried.

Dink looked out the window again. "It's Hanna!" he said.

Alice and the kids ran outside. Hanna was standing next to the picnic table. On the ground by her feet were a tray, a pitcher, and four plastic drinking glasses. She was crying and shaking her head. Alice grabbed Hanna in a hug. "Honey,

what is it?" she asked. "What happened?"

Hanna wiped her eyes. "It . . . it was under the table!" she said, pointing. "It ran right over my foot!"

"What ran over your foot?" Alice asked.

"A rattlesnake!" Hanna said.

"Goodness!" Alice said. "Did it bite you?"

"No, it slithered away," Hanna said, holding Alice's hand.

Just then, Howie came running. "What's going on?" he asked. Bear showed up and started lapping at the spilled lemonade.

"Hanna saw a rattlesnake under the table!" Alice said.

Howie looked to where Alice was pointing.

"Are there really rattlesnakes around here?" Josh asked.

"Yup, but I've never seen one," Howie said. "They're shy and keep out of sight."

Hanna bent to pick up the tray. "Leave that," Alice said. "We'll take care of it. You go in the house and relax. Maybe check on my cookies?"

Hanna hurried across the yard to the house.

"What other poisonous snakes live in

Florida?" Ruth Rose asked Howie.

"We have several," he said. "The ones I know about are rattlesnakes, water moccasins, copperheads, and coral snakes. *Those* are the pretty ones—the coral snakes. They have red, yellow, and black bands around their bodies, like ribbons."

Everyone looked at the ground.

"Do any poisonous ones come near the bunkhouse?" Josh asked.

Howie shook his head. "Not likely. If a snake sees a human or a dog, it'll hide," he said. "Plus, we have skunks and raccoons around here, and the snakes are afraid of them, too."

"Skunks?" Josh whispered.

"I'll clean up this lemonade stuff," Howie offered.

"Thanks, you're a dear," Alice said. "Come on, kids."

Alice unlocked the padlock and slid the barn door open. When the kids stepped inside, dim blue lights came on.

"Wow!" Josh said.

The inside of the barn had been turned into a night sky. All four walls, the ceiling, and the floor were painted dark blue with bright stars. Planets hung from the ceiling on thin wires. A large white moon had been painted on the back wall. In front of the moon stood cutouts of three astronauts in space suits.

"This is incredible!" Dink said. He

spun around, trying to take it all in. "It's like being . . . in outer space!"

Alice twisted a dimmer switch on the wall, and the lights got brighter. "My husband worked for Kennedy Space Center. He and some of his engineer friends built it all in their spare time."

"What's that?" Ruth Rose asked. She was pointing at a twenty-foot-tall metal contraption leaning against a wall. One side was open, and leather seats were visible. A ladder was attached to one side.

"That's a small replica of a space shuttle," Alice told her. "My husband saw the real ones at Kennedy Space Center."

Josh was looking up at a silver tube hanging from the ceiling by cables. It was the same length as the space shuttle. "Is that a submarine?" he asked Alice.

"It's a space simulator," Alice said. "Barney made that, too. It moves forward and backward and rolls from side to side, making you think you're traveling in space with no gravity!"

"I definitely have to try that!" Ruth Rose said. "How do you get up there?"

Alice pointed to a switch on the wall. "I can lower it, and there are buttons inside to control the thing. Howie's kids love playing astronaut in it!"

"Why did your husband build all this?" Dink asked.

Alice smiled. "He was a space nut,"

she said. "Always regretted he couldn't go into space. So he started building and collecting stuff."

She walked over to a small desk in one corner. "This is where Barney wrote in his diary," she said. "He also sent letters to scientists, and a lot of them wrote back to him. He kept the letters in a fat folder. Now the folder's gone, along with his diary and pen." She pulled open the desk drawer. It was empty.

"Why was he writing to scientists?" Dink asked.

"Barney was concerned about the environment," Alice said. "He walked this property every day, taking notes. He even made trails through that jungle out there. Then he wrote to scientists at NASA and the Space Center with his ideas: how to turn Spanish moss into food for cattle, how to use pond algae for running cars, how to bring in seaweed from the coast to fertilize crops."

On the desk was a green blotter stained with ink. A jar of pencils sat on the blotter. Taped to the jar was a sign that said BARNEY'S STUFF.

Josh pulled a shiny pen from the jar. "Is this your husband's pen?" he asked.

"Oh my goodness, it is!" Alice said. She grabbed the pen and gave Josh a hug. "My eyesight!"

The little sign on the jar caused a thought to pop into Dink's mind. Then it popped out again. He closed his eyes, trying to remember something he'd noticed earlier. Dink felt it was important, but he couldn't bring the thought back.

Around the huge room were displays of space suits and packages of the food astronauts ate while in space. Autographed pictures of at least twenty astronauts hung on one wall. Samples of moon rocks were lined up on a shelf.

"Did those really come from the moon?" Ruth Rose asked.

"They sure did," Alice said. "Astronaut Neil Armstrong gathered rocks when he walked on the moon." She pointed to one rock. "See, he signed this one."

"What's this?" Josh asked. He was standing at a plastic display case. Inside was a strange-looking object shaped like a capital letter H. It was about four feet long, and sat on a sheet of plywood lying across two wooden trestles. Part was cut away to show compartments inside it.

"There are itty-bitty people inside!" Josh said.

"That's my husband's replica of the International Space Station," Alice said.

She pointed up. "The real one is up in the sky right now, with real astronauts living in it!"

Josh peered inside the miniature space station. "What do astronauts in space eat?" he asked.

"From what I hear, nothing very tasty," Alice said, heading for the door. "But *you* get to eat some of my famous cookies!"

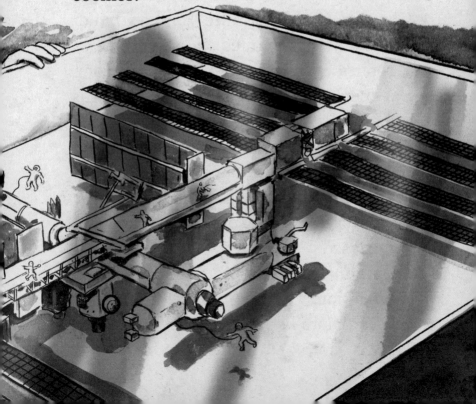

CHAPTER 5

The kids followed Alice back to the house. They stopped to admire Hanna's motor scooter. It was painted the same blue as a robin's egg. There were two side compartments under the rear seat. One was open and held books. The cover of one of the books showed a woman who was an old-timey movie star. The word *FILM* was printed in silvery letters beneath the actress's face. The other compartment was closed.

Hanna had left the scooter's key in the ignition. The key was on a thin chain holding more keys.

"I'm getting a scooter like this someday!" Josh said. "Here's where I'll keep my snacks." He tapped the closed compartment.

"Get one that holds three people," Ruth Rose said. "You can drive Dink and me around town!" She bent down and plucked a limp flower that was stuck in the front wheel spokes. "This flower matches my outfit!"

They went inside, where the kitchen smelled like warm cookies. Wallis and Hanna were sitting at the table, drinking lemonade.

Ruth Rose put her flower in a small glass of water and set it on the table.

"Everyone sit," Alice said. She arranged some cookies on a plate and brought it to the table. "Help yourselves!"

"Hanna was telling me about the rattlesnake," Wallis said. "I would have screamed and dropped the lemonade, too!"

"Not me," Josh said, reaching for a cookie. "I love snakes!"

"And snakes love you," Dink added.

Everyone laughed and began eating Alice's cookies.

Hanna stood up and put her glass in the sink. "I'm going to go study with Kenny," she said. She took two cookies off the plate and left by the back door.

"I think Hanna and Kenny are

sweethearts," Alice said. "They spend a lot of time together."

"Do they go to the same school?" Wallis asked.

Alice nodded. "They both go to the community college, but I let them study here because it's a lot quieter than their dorm," she said. "Hanna wants to be a movie producer!"

"Awesome!" Josh said. "Maybe she can make a movie of one of your books, Wallis."

"Lovely idea," Wallis said. "Why don't you kids do some exploring before supper? Uncle Barney found some arrowheads in the dirt behind the barn, right, Auntie?"

"He sure did," Alice said. "There are shovels in the toolshed behind the café. But stay away from the pond."

"You might want to put on some mosquito repellent," Wallis suggested.

"I have some in my backpack," Ruth Rose said.

Alice stood up. "Goodness, it's almost five o'clock!" She covered the plate of cookies with aluminum foil and handed it to Ruth Rose. "Give these to Howie, would you?" she asked. "His kids will be upset if he doesn't bring some of my cookies home!"

Dink took his glass to the sink and

placed it next to Hanna's, glancing at the magnets on the fridge door. The alligator's mouth was empty—the note was gone. But he remembered the lost thought that had been bothering him. He opened the drawer in front of him, picked up what was inside, and slipped it into his back pocket.

The kids trooped out the back door. "Remind me to tell you something later," Dink whispered to Josh and Ruth Rose.

In the yard, Bear appeared from around the corner of the house, followed by Howie.

Bear ran up to Ruth Rose to sniff what she was carrying.

"Are those cookies, by any chance?" Howie asked.

Ruth Rose handed over the plate. "Auntie Alice said they're for your kids," she said. "Can we meet them?"

"Sure," he said. "I'll bring Maddy and Seth over tomorrow. They have a school project to do, and I said I'd help them."

"A space project?" Dink asked.

Howie shook his head. "Nope. It's about animals," he said, walking toward his van.

"What kind of animals?" Josh asked.

"Think paws and claws," Howie said.

Dink, Josh, and Ruth Rose watched him drive away.

"Great," Josh muttered. "We just missed running into a mountain lion. There are bats in the trees, scorpions in the beds, and alligators in the pond! Snakes are hiding under picnic tables!"

Dink laughed. "But Ruth Rose and I are here to protect you," he said.

"Guys, if we're going to look for arrowheads, we need to do it before it gets dark," Ruth Rose said. "Let's get my mosquito spray."

The kids went inside the bunkhouse and sprayed Pine Shine over their clothes.

It smelled like a Christmas tree. Dink tossed *Super Science* onto his bunk, and then they found shovels and a rake in the toolshed.

"What did you want to tell us?" Josh asked Dink.

"When we first got here, there was a note on the fridge," Dink told his friends. "It said something about buying paper towels, and was signed *H*. I figure Hanna or Howie wrote it to Auntie A."

Josh stared at Dink. "That's it?" he asked. "Paper towels?"

"No," Dink said. "I'm pretty sure the handwriting was the same as on that postcard Auntie Alice got today."

"The one from somebody wanting to buy her house?" Ruth Rose asked. "Why would the handwriting be the same?"

"That's what I want to know," Dink said. He showed them the postcard he'd snitched from the kitchen.

"Couldn't be the same," Josh said. "The writer wants to buy the house. The note writer is either Hanna or Howie, asking Auntie A. to buy paper towels!"

"I could be wrong," Dink said. "And the note is gone, so I can't compare them. Anyway, let's look for arrowheads."

They walked behind the barn. The algae covering the pond looked thick and slimy. Dink remembered the magazine cover. Was *algae* the green goo that was going to save the planet?

"I wonder if there really is an alligator in the pond," Josh said. "Don't get too close, guys."

"Lots of animals come here to drink," Ruth Rose said.

"Very funny, Bunny," Josh said.

"Josh, I wasn't trying to be funny," Ruth Rose said. "Come look at these tracks."

Josh and Dink walked over to where she was standing. There were prints in the dark, wet ground. Most were tiny, like the ones birds or small animals would make.

But Dink noticed wide prints with four long toes.

CHAPTER 6

The kids looked down at the tracks. "These could be from a bear," Ruth Rose said. "Black bears eat fish, and fish live in ponds like this."

"I'm going home," Josh said.

"It's a long walk to Connecticut," Dink said.

Ruth Rose stepped a few feet away. "Guys, check this out," she said.

Dink and Josh joined her. "What?" Dink asked.

"More tracks," Ruth Rose said. "Only these are human."

A couple of feet from the water were

several shoe prints. "I wonder who was walking here," Dink said.

"Maybe Kenny and Hanna," Ruth Rose suggested.

"Or the burglars!" Josh said.

Dink stared at the footprints. "Why would anybody hang out here, where it's muddy and smelly?" He swatted at a mosquito. "And buggy!"

"Maybe they got too close, and the alligator got them!" Josh said.

"Well, we came out to look for arrowheads," Ruth Rose said. She walked away with the rake and began scraping the dirt next to the barn.

Dink and Josh started digging holes with their shovels.

Ten minutes later, they had a small pile of treasures they'd dug up: three tin cans, the broken handle of a coffee mug, a green bottle, a horseshoe, and seven rusty nails.

"Not one arrowhead," Dink said.

"Maybe Wallis's uncle found them all," Josh said. "Anyway, it's getting dark. We can try again tomorrow."

They put the shovels and rake inside the toolshed and closed the door.

"I need to wash my hands," Ruth Rose said. The kids headed around the corner of the barn, toward the bunkhouse. Kenny and Hanna were sitting at the picnic table with books in front of them, but they weren't reading.

"Hey," Kenny said when he noticed the kids. "What's going on?"

The kids walked over to say hi. "We were looking for arrowheads," Dink said.

Kenny sprayed himself and Hanna with a can of Bug Off! The smell was strong and made Dink's eyes water. "Find any?" Kenny asked.

"Just a lot of junk," Josh said.

"Bummer," Kenny said. He was tapping his fingers on the cover of his book. *Botany* was printed on the front.

"What are you reading about?" Josh asked, pointing at the title.

"The study of plants," Kenny said. "Trust me, there are a zillion kinds of plants in Florida."

"What about algae? We saw a lot of algae on the pond," Dink said.

"Man, I wouldn't go near any of the ponds!" Kenny said. "I saw rattlesnakes near them last week. And I'm pretty sure there're gators, too."

"How many ponds are there?" Dink asked. "We only saw one."

"There are more back in the jungle," Kenny said. "But I wouldn't go out there, either." He grinned. "Unless you like snakes and spiders."

"Did you really see a mountain lion here this morning?" Josh asked.

"Yup," Kenny said.

"Auntie Alice said you took a picture," Ruth Rose said. "Could we see it?"

Kenny opened his phone and tapped a few buttons. "Here it is," he said. He held his phone so all three kids could see the screen.

In the photo, a tan-colored mountain lion lay stretched out in the middle of the driveway. Its long tail was curled near its back legs. Behind the animal, Dink could see the barn.

Dink looked closer. "Where are the

cars?" he asked. "They're not in the driveway."

"Cars? Oh, Howie was going to wash the cars, so I guess he moved them out front, near the hose," Kenny said.

Just then, they all heard someone calling. "It's Wallis," Ruth Rose said.

"I hope it's suppertime!" Josh said.

The kids ran to the house and into the kitchen. The table was set with five places. Platters of food were lined up on the counter. Bear was under the table, slapping his tail against the floor.

"Grab a plate and help yourselves," Alice said. "After you wash your hands!"

Alice and Wallis served fried chicken, mashed potatoes, and green beans. For dessert, there were three flavors of ice cream.

After the table was cleared, they played Scrabble. Then the kids headed back to the barn.

Two hours later, the kids were in their bunks. They had left the bunkhouse windows up to let breezes come through the screens. Crickets and frogs made chirping and cheeping noises.

"My stomach hurts," Josh said from his bottom bunk. He was wearing Spider-Man pajamas.

"You ate seconds of everything," Ruth Rose said. "Like a hungry badger."

"Guys, did you notice anything weird about Kenny's picture of the mountain lion?" Dink asked. He was lying on his upper bunk, gazing out the window.

"Weird how?" Josh asked.

"Well, for one thing, this morning Kenny told us the lion was near the station wagon in the driveway," Dink said. "But I didn't see any cars in that picture he took."

"He told us Howie probably moved the cars to wash them," Ruth Rose said from her bunk. "Maybe the lion got there after he moved them."

Dink sat up. "Okay, but he said the hose was out front," he said. "The hose isn't there, though. It's behind the bunkhouse."

No answers came.

"Another thing," Dink continued. "The picture shows the barn in the background. But in the picture, the barn door isn't painted with that cool space shuttle. Auntie A. told us Howie painted it last week. So if Kenny took the picture this morning, how come the barn door wasn't painted?"

"Maybe Auntie Alice is confused about when the lion was in the driveway," Ruth Rose said. "Or Kenny got it mixed up."

Dink shook his head. "They both said the lion was there this morning," he said.

"Why would Kenny lie about that?" Josh asked.

Dink thought. "Maybe he was lying to Auntie A.," he said.

"But why?" Josh asked.

"Remember I thought the note on the fridge signed by H. had the same handwriting as that postcard Auntie A. got today?" Dink asked. "If I'm right, it might mean that either Hanna or Howie wrote the note *and* the postcards. And then if Kenny is lying about the mountain lion, it could mean the three of them are trying to get Auntie A. to sell her house."

"But the postcard was signed *M.K.*," Ruth Rose said. "Who's that?"

"I know," Dink muttered. "I mean I don't know."

"It does seem weird that it's all happening at the same time," Josh said. "Postcards and phone calls trying to buy her house, rattlesnakes and mountain lions in her yard, and a burglar taking her husband's stuff."

"It feels like someone is trying to scare Auntie A.," Ruth Rose said.

"Well, they're scaring *me!*" Josh said.

"Whatever's going on," Dink said, "my Dink brain is telling me someone's really anxious to get this place away from Auntie A."

"But Howie and Kenny and Hanna are Auntie's *friends*," Ruth Rose said.

"I know they are," Dink said, getting under his covers. "And they all know where she keeps her key to the barn."

Just as Dink was dropping off to sleep, he felt Josh kick the bottom of his bunk. "Dink!" Josh whispered. "Are you awake?"

"I am now," Dink said. "What do you want?"

"My Josh brain just asked me a question."

Dink grinned. "What did your Josh brain ask you?" he said. "And why does it have to ask right now?"

"It asked me why the burglar didn't steal anything valuable from the barn," Josh said. "Like those moon rocks and those signed pictures of the astronauts. They must be worth something, right?"

Dink thought about that. Josh was right. All the burglars took were a diary and some old letters. "See you in the morning," he told Josh.

CHAPTER 7

Dink opened his eyes. Something had awakened him. He tried to see around him, but the bunkhouse was dark. It was quiet outside. Even the crickets had stopped making their night sounds.

Then Dink heard something creak. He sat up and looked toward the door.

Dink knew the hinges squeaked when the screen door opened and closed. But who would be opening it in the middle of the night? And Dink was almost certain that Josh had latched the door before climbing into his bunk.

But he wasn't 100 percent positive.

So he threw off his blanket and climbed down the bunk's ladder. Josh was snoring.

As Dink's feet reached the floor, he smelled mosquito repellent. But it didn't have a pine scent like Ruth Rose's. This was stronger—and familiar.

Praying that he wouldn't step on a scorpion, Dink walked to the door and peered out. He saw a few stars, but the moon was behind some clouds. The air was warm and damp. Flying insects bumped into the screen.

Dink ran his hand along the wooden frame of the screen door, feeling for the hook-and-eye latch. His fingers found the hook, but it was hanging loose, not latched.

He stood there for a minute, trying to remember what Josh had said last night. Something about *locking the door to keep the wild critters out!*

So if Josh had latched the door, why was it not latched now? Dink dropped the hook into the round little eye and pushed the door to make sure it wouldn't open.

Dink tiptoed back to the bunk bed and climbed the ladder. He shivered and pulled his blanket up under his chin. Closing his eyes, he convinced himself that no animal had come into the bunkhouse. But who had unlatched the door?

Sunlight coming through the window shone in Dink's eyes, waking him. He blinked, yawned, and sat up. He looked at the pond and some palm trees through the window. Then he glanced around the bunkhouse.

Below him, Josh was a lump under a blanket with one foot sticking out, dangling over the floor. Dink smiled. Josh had taken his shoes off, but had slept in his socks.

Across the room, Ruth Rose was also snuggled beneath the covers. No bears, wolves, or mountain lions were there, unless they were hiding in the bathroom. He checked his watch—it was seven-thirty. Yawning, he reached for the magazine Auntie A. had lent him.

He read part of an article about how the earth was getting warmer. He read about scientists trying to turn algae into fuel. Auntie A.'s husband had written to scientists about a similar idea. Dink looked up at the ceiling. Maybe Barney Wallace was onto something!

Dink's stomach growled. He dropped the magazine, wondering what they'd be having for breakfast. He pulled his toothbrush and toothpaste from his backpack and climbed down the ladder. The wood floor felt cool on his bare feet. *I should've kept my socks on, too,* he thought.

He took a step toward the bathroom, then froze.

Ten inches from Josh's foot, a snake was curled up between Dink's sneakers.

Dink backed up, bumping Josh's bed.

"What're you doing?" Josh mumbled.

"There's a snake on the floor," Dink whispered. "Don't move!"

Josh snorted. "Don't play games, James," he said.

Dink climbed halfway up his ladder. "I'm not!" he said. "Take a look and you'll see it, about a foot from your bunk!"

Josh peeked out from his blanket and gasped.

"What's going on?" Ruth Rose said suddenly. She was sitting up, rubbing her eyes.

"Don't get out of bed," Dink said. "There's a snake on the floor by my sneakers."

"OH MY GOSH!" Ruth Rose cried. "What's it doing there?"

"I don't know," Dink said.

"How did it get in here?" Josh asked. Only his eyes and nose were visible from under his blanket.

"Josh, did you lock the screen door last night?" Dink asked.

"Yup," Josh said. "Why?"

"Because I got up during the night,

and the door *wasn't* latched!"

Josh moaned.

"It's not moving," Ruth Rose said. "Maybe it's a fake snake."

"Nope, I just saw its little tongue come out," Josh said. "It's real!"

"Guys, it has red, yellow, and black bands," Ruth Rose said. "IT'S A POISONOUS CORAL SNAKE!"

The three kids watched the snake, but it wasn't doing anything. It lay curled up with its head resting on the toe of Dink's sneaker. Every few seconds, a thin tongue shot out of its mouth. It had tiny eyes, which didn't blink.

"We need a plan," Ruth Rose said.

"I *have* a plan," Josh said. "Strap me in that space shuttle, and shoot me up to the moon. I'll hang out with Blinky!"

"We'll be fine as long as we stay in bed," Dink said. "I don't think snakes can jump."

"Dude, if this snake unlocked the

door, it can climb into my bunk!" Josh
said.

"I have an idea," Ruth Rose said. She
stretched one foot out from under her
blanket. Using her toes, she dragged the
wire trash basket to the side of her bed.
She sat up and grabbed the basket.

"What are you doing?" Josh hissed.

Ruth Rose tiptoed across the room
and quickly dropped the wastebasket
over the snake and Dink's sneakers. The
snake moved, but too late. It was a pris-
oner inside the basket's wire mesh.

"Now it can't get us!" Ruth Rose announced.

"And I can't get my sneakers," Dink said.

Josh giggled. "Snakes love bare feet, Pete!" he said. "Thanks, Ruth Rose. You're a rock star!"

Dink climbed back down the ladder. He knelt to get a good look at the snake. "It's kind of pretty," Dink said. "I like its little red face."

"What should we do with it?" Ruth Rose asked.

Dink thought for a minute. "Hey, remember when Kenny was driving us here and we passed Snake World?" he asked. "We could bring the snake over there!"

"Great idea," Josh said. "You take the snake while I eat a pancake!"

CHAPTER 8

After dressing in shorts and T-shirts, the kids brushed their teeth and left the bunk-house. The snake seemed to be sleeping.

Dink stopped to look at the hook-and-eye latch hanging on the screen door frame. When he ran his fingers over the screen, he noticed something else.

He got down on his knees to see if a snake could fit under the door. The space between the door and the floor was less than the thickness of his finger. Dink didn't think the snake could have squeezed through there. Besides, he'd heard the hinges creak, which meant the screen door had opened. A snake couldn't unlatch and open a door!

The kids went to the house for breakfast. They told Wallis and her aunt about the snake.

"Goodness!" Auntie Alice said. "I've never seen a snake near the house or bunkhouse. Then suddenly two in a row show up!"

Dink said he thought they should call Snake World.

Wallis pulled her cell phone from a pocket. "They must have a website," she said.

"Good," Alice said. "I want that critter gone before Howie brings his kids over!"

Wallis found and tapped the number. "It's ringing. I'm putting it on speaker so you can hear," she told her aunt and the three kids.

"Snake World," a man's voice said.

"Hello, I'm calling from Alice Wallace's home," Wallis said. "We're just down the road. We found a coral snake on the property this morning, and we don't know what to do with it."

"How do you know it's a coral snake?" the man asked.

"It has red, yellow, and black bands around its body," Wallis said.

The phone was quiet for a few seconds. Then the man said, "What color is the snake's head?"

Wallis looked at the kids and raised her eyebrows.

"Red," Dink said.

"Well, that's good news," the man said. "Coral snakes have black heads. What you have is most likely a *scarlet king snake*. They resemble coral snakes, but they're totally harmless. Tell you what, I'll come over and have a look. Ten minutes okay?"

"That would be great!" Wallis said. "Fifty-three Palm Lane. It's the white house with black shutters."

While they finished breakfast, Ruth Rose opened her guidebook to the section about Florida wildlife. She quickly found pictures of a coral snake and a scarlet king snake. Side by side, they looked almost alike. But the coral snake's red and yellow bands touched each other, and the scarlet king snake had a red head.

She turned the book so everyone could see the page.

"Good," Dink said. "I can get my sneakers back!"

A horn tooted. They all went outside, where a truck sat in the driveway. SNAKE WORLD was printed on the door. A guy in jeans and a Snake World T-shirt stepped out. "I'm Jake," the man said. "Heard you folks got yourself a visitor!"

Ruth Rose showed him the picture of the scarlet king snake. "We think it's this one," she said.

"Hope you're right," Jake said. He pulled a cloth sack from his back pocket and put on a pair of thick gloves.

Jake followed the kids, Wallis, and Alice to the bunkhouse. They crowded around the overturned wastebasket.

Jake got down on his knees and handed each kid a pair of gloves. Dink slipped the gloves over his hands and waited.

"Lift the basket," Jake said quietly. Dink pulled the basket away, and Jake grabbed the snake. He held it on his knee while stroking the shiny scales on its back.

"Definitely not a coral snake," he said, pointing to the red face and head. "Coral snakes and scarlet king snakes both have red, yellow, and black markings. People confuse them all the time. But the three colors are arranged differently. Here's a rhyme to help you remember which is which: *If red touches yellow, he's a dangerous fellow. If red touches black, you're safe, Jack.*"

"Cool," Josh said. "You're a poet!"

"Notice how this snake's red bands touch the black bands but not the yellow ones," Jake went on.

"Can I hold it?" Ruth Rose asked.

"Sure," Jake said. "Support its neck with one hand, and put the other under its belly." He gently placed the snake in Ruth Rose's hands. "How does it feel?"

"Amazing," Ruth Rose whispered. "All smooth and shiny."

Dink ran a finger down the snake's side. "I can feel its muscles moving inside," he said. "Want to touch it, Josh?"

"No. Maybe. Okay." Josh put a finger on the snake's skin. "Nice snake, Jake," he said.

Jake laughed and slid the snake into the bag. "If y'all want to come by Snake World, I can show you a coral snake up close," he said. "But you won't have to touch it."

"Maybe we'll do that before we leave," Wallis said. "But I have an idea these kids want to go into outer space today, right?"

"Right!" the three kids yelled.

WELCOME TO THE SPACE SHUTTLE

CHAPTER 9

"It's perfectly safe," Alice told Wallis and the three kids. "Howie's kids play in it all the time."

The space simulator was resting on the barn floor with its clear plastic hatch open. There were three seats in the cockpit. Ruth Rose sat in the front seat, with Dink behind her. Josh was squeezed in behind him. Their knees were bent so they could fit in the small seats.

"It's like being on a toboggan," Josh said. "With no snow!"

"You ready to go up in space?" Alice asked them.

"What if I get sick?" Josh asked.

"Don't even think about it," Dink said. "We're ready!"

Wallis slid the hatch halfway closed. "Push the red button!" she said through the opening. "I'm going to take a video!"

Ruth Rose touched the red button, and the cables rose, pulling the tube toward the ceiling. When the simulator stopped moving upward, she pushed the green button. They began to rock forward and backward.

"Oh my gosh!" Josh yelled.

Then the tube began to roll from side to side, making all three kids burst out laughing.

"Blinky, here we come!" Dink yelled.

"If you squint your eyes," Ruth Rose said, "you'll really think you're in space!"

Dink looked down and saw Wallis with her cell phone aimed at the simulator. The kids waved at her.

They stayed "in space" for a while, and then Ruth Rose pushed the white button. The tube stopped swaying. When she touched the red button, they returned to the barn floor. Wallis slid the hatch open, and the kids climbed out.

"I have a great video!" Wallis said. She played the video on her phone. There was the silver tube against the dark blue background. It seemed to be sailing through the sky.

"That is so cool!" Josh said. "The stars painted on the ceiling, with the planets hanging down, made it really look like space!"

Then they walked over to the space shuttle and got inside. Ruth Rose was in front, where she read to Dink and Josh from a card taped on the dashboard. It told how in July 1969, the Apollo 11 mission took astronauts Neil Armstrong, Buzz Aldrin, and Michael Collins to the moon. Armstrong and Aldrin walked on the moon for three hours. They took pictures, gathered samples, and planted a U.S. flag.

"It took them three days to get to the

moon from Kennedy Space Center," Ruth Rose said.

"How did the astronauts get home?" Josh asked.

Ruth Rose read from the card. "They came back on July 24," she said. "They were in a special capsule that landed in the Pacific Ocean! A helicopter picked them up."

"Wow," Josh said.

Just then, the barn door opened. A boy and girl ran inside and stopped when they saw the three older kids. Howie came in, carrying a backpack. Bear was with them, jumping up to lick the kids' fingers.

Dink, Josh, and Ruth Rose climbed down from the shuttle to meet the new kids.

"These are Maddy and Seth," Howie said. "And these visitors are from Connecticut. Shake hands, y'all!"

Dink, Josh, and Ruth Rose introduced

themselves, and they all shook hands.

"Maddy and Seth are twins," Howie said. "They were born seven years ago next week."

"And we're going to Disney World for our birthday, right, Dad?" Seth asked.

The twins were dressed alike, in green shorts and white T-shirts. Seth was holding a rubber snake, and Bear was trying to take it from his hand.

"Maybe we'll go to Disney World, if you stop chasing your sister with that snake," his father said. He held up the backpack. "Let's go to the pond and see what we can find."

The five kids followed Howie out of the barn. Bear ran in circles around them, barking in excitement. Dink noticed Kenny and Hanna walking away from the picnic table. They stopped talking when the kids and Howie walked past.

Behind the barn, Howie opened the backpack. He took out a jar of water, a bag that said PLASTER OF PARIS, a plastic cup and bowl, and a wooden mixing spoon.

"We're doing a nature project for school," Seth said.

"What kind of project?" Josh asked.

"Making animal tracks," Maddy said.

Howie led Bear to a shady spot next to the barn and told him to stay. Bear whined, but he lay down with his chin on his front paws.

"A hungry alligator will jump right out of the water and grab a little dog," Howie told the kids. "But I've never seen one here."

Josh pointed to one of the large tracks they'd seen yesterday. "Is that a bear track?" he asked Howie.

"That's a good print for our project," Howie said. "But it's not from a bear. Bear feet are much wider than these. And bears have long, curved claws. When they walk, the claws make pointy marks in the dirt."

He pointed at the print. "You can see a few toenail marks here, but if these were bear tracks, the claw marks would be deeper and bigger. I'm guessing this track came from a large dog," Howie said. "Maybe a coyote or wolf."

"How do you know so much about animals?" Josh asked.

Howie smiled. "I worked in a zoo when I was in high school," he said. "And I read everything I can find about wildlife."

"Could this track be from the mountain lion that Kenny saw?" Ruth Rose asked.

"When was that?" Howie asked.

Dink thought a minute. "Yesterday morning," he said. "Kenny said it was in the driveway."

"I washed Ms. Wallace's car yesterday morning before I started cleaning the gutters," he said. "I didn't see any mountain lion."

"Did you move the cars to wash them?" Dink asked.

"Nope, the bunkhouse hose reached fine."

Howie knelt and put his finger on the dog print. "Anyway, this isn't from a mountain lion," he said. "Cats, including the big ones, keep their claws folded inside their paws when they walk. They don't leave claw marks in the dirt, like a dog or bear would."

"Do you think the mountain lion

will come back?" Josh asked. He looked nervous.

Howie shrugged. "Probably not," he said. "They'd rather hunt for their food where there are no humans around." He gestured toward the thick trees and bushes around the pond. "Like back there, where the foxes and raccoons live."

"Is that Auntie A.'s land, too?" Dink asked.

"Yup. She owns a mile or so back there," Howie said. "Mostly jungle and ponds, but it's worth a fortune. She told me about the folks bugging her to sell, but I told her to hold on. Land only gets more valuable!"

Howie pointed across the pond. "Her husband started to cut trails through once, but I reckon it's grown over now," he said.

"Dad, when can we do it?" Seth asked. He stuffed his rubber snake in a pocket of his shorts.

"Right now!" his father said. Following his directions, the kids poured one cup of plaster into the plastic bowl. They added two cups of water and stirred the mixture until it looked like thick white soup. They poured it into the deep paw print.

"Now we wait for the plaster to harden," Howie said.

Seth and Maddy made casts of some of the smaller animal prints while everyone waited for the plaster in the deep paw print to harden. Howie pointed out the differences between raccoon, opossum, and fox prints.

After about twenty minutes, they went back to the first cast. The plaster had hardened, so Howie lifted it from the ground. He brushed off a clump of mud. The result was a perfect dog track.

"Who wants some lunch?" said Wallis from behind them.

CHAPTER 10

The five kids and Howie washed the plaster and mud off each other's hands with the hose. Alice and Wallis brought sandwiches, apples, cookies, and lemonade to the picnic table.

"Bear, go under, please," Auntie Alice told her dog. Bear crawled under the picnic table and flopped on the grass.

They had a noisy lunch, with Dink, Josh, Ruth Rose, Seth, and Maddy all showing off their plaster animal tracks. Seth's rubber snake sat on the table, and everybody pretended to be afraid of it.

When the last sandwich had been

eaten, Howie stood up. "Okay, Seth and Maddy," he said. "We told Mom we'd help her in the garden, so we'd better get on home. Tell everyone thank you."

Seth and Maddy collected their plaster prints, said thank you, and raced to their dad's van. Bear ran after them, barking. Dink, Josh, and Ruth Rose helped Alice and Wallis bring the lunch stuff into the kitchen.

Hanna's motor scooter roared up the driveway, with Kenny driving. Hanna sat behind him with her hands on his shoulders.

Through the kitchen door, Dink watched them walk toward the picnic table with their books. Hanna sprayed Kenny with insect repellent, and they both laughed.

"Let's meet in the bunkhouse," Dink whispered to Josh and Ruth Rose. He left the kitchen and walked across the yard. Kenny and Hanna were sitting at the table with their books open. They were watching Dink, so he waved.

Josh and Ruth Rose came through the bunkhouse screen door a minute later, each munching on a cookie. Josh handed one to Dink, who was sitting on Josh's bunk.

Josh plopped next to him, and Ruth Rose sat on the upside-down wastebasket. "You have that look on your face," she said to Dink.

"Tell all, Paul," Josh said, bumping Dink's shoulder with his own.

"I think I figured out how that snake got inside the bunkhouse," Dink said. He walked over to the door and pointed to a small hole in the screen, about two inches from the hook-and-eye latch.

"I noticed the hole this morning," Dink told them.

"You think the snake crawled through that?" Josh asked.

"No," Dink said. "Remember I found

the door unlatched last night? I think someone undid the hook from the outside."

He took a pencil from his backpack, walked outside, and let the screen door close behind him. "Latch it," he told Josh.

Josh slipped the hook into the eye. "Okay, it's locked," he said.

"Now watch," Dink said. He slid the pencil through the hole and lifted the hook out of the eye. "Now it's unlocked."

"Wow!" Josh said.

"They couldn't lock it again when they left," Dink went on. "That's why it was unhooked when I got up last night."

"But why would anyone want to get in here?" Josh asked. "We don't have anything to steal."

"The person who opened the door didn't want to take anything," Dink said. "They wanted to *leave* something—the snake."

Josh and Ruth Rose stared at Dink.

Josh's mouth fell open. "Who would do such a lousy thing?" he finally managed to ask.

Dink shook his head. "I'm betting on Kenny or Hanna," he said. "When I got up last night, I smelled that awful insect repellent they use. I think putting a snake in here was part of a plan to scare Auntie A. so she'd sell her property."

"But why would any of them want this place that bad?" Josh asked. "It's just an old house and a barn."

"Maybe it's more," Dink said. "The postcards and phone calls started coming in after Auntie A.'s husband's diary and letters were stolen. So maybe he wrote something important."

"Auntie A. told us her husband used to explore all this property," Ruth Rose said. "Maybe he found something!"

"Yup, and if Hanna saw his diary when she was cleaning in the barn, she might have read it and found out what he wrote," Dink said. "Then she and her boyfriend came up with a plan to get the property away from Auntie A."

"Do you think Howie is helping Kenny and Hanna?" Josh asked.

"Nope. He told Auntie A. not to sell yet," Dink reminded Josh and Ruth Rose. "So he can't be one of the people trying to get it away from her."

"We need to find that diary," Ruth Rose said. "Then we'll know what Hanna and Kenny know!"

"Yeah, but if they hid it somewhere, we'll never find it," Dink said. "It's probably in one of their lockers at college."

"In TV shows, the good stuff is always in a safe-deposit box in a bank," Josh said. "And the detective finds a mysterious key in the dead guy's pocket and—"

"That's TV," Ruth Rose said. "But Hanna has keys. I saw them. Hey, maybe the diary is in one of the compartments on her scooter!"

"We can't take her keys or search her bike," Dink said. "But we can check out the rest of this property. Maybe we'll find what makes Hanna and Kenny so anxious to get it."

"You want to explore a jungle?" Josh said. "With bugs and snakes and alligators?"

"Have you guys noticed that Kenny is the only person who saw alligators on this property?" Dink asked. "He also said he saw a mountain lion, but no one else did. Hanna said she saw a rattlesnake, but no one else saw it, either. I think they're lying."

"All to scare Auntie A.," Ruth Rose said.

"They're trying to scare you and me and Josh, too," Dink said.

"Why?" Josh asked.

"Because they don't want us to go near the ponds," Dink said. He found Ruth Rose's Pine Shine and held it up. "Let's go find out why."

CHAPTER 11

The kids put on jeans, long-sleeved shirts, and baseball caps. They sprayed the repellent over their clothes. Then they left the bunkhouse and headed toward the jungle behind the barn.

"Wait a minute," Josh said. He ran to the toolshed and came back with a rake.

"What's that for?" Dink asked.

"Critter protection," Josh said.

They walked slowly around the pond. In the muddy places, they spotted more animal tracks. Josh carried his rake like a spear.

They split up, each peering through

the underbrush for signs of the old trails Alice had told them about. Josh poked his rake into dark places. Dink kept an eye on the algae-covered pond, hoping some swamp creature wasn't watching *them*.

"Guys, I think I found something!" Ruth Rose called. She was twenty yards away with her back to the pond and the barn.

Dink and Josh ran over. Ruth Rose pointed at a small white circle on the trunk of an oak tree.

"That's paint," Josh said. "And it's faded, so it's old."

"Maybe Auntie A.'s husband put it there," Ruth Rose said.

"Let's look for more," Dink said. The kids stepped past the tree. Josh poked his rake into bushes.

"There!" Dink said, pointing just ahead of them. A few yards from the first marked tree was another faded white circle. "I think we've found the trail!"

The kids walked deeper into the woods. Thick bushes brushed against their arms and faces. Mosquitoes buzzed around them, but didn't land. Behind them, the pond and barn were no longer visible. Tree branches blocked out the sun.

Every few yards, they found another white circle on a tree trunk. The marks drew the kids farther into a jungle-like place.

"I feel like tigers are watching us,"
Josh whispered.

"Tigers don't live in Florida," Ruth
Rose said.

"Yeah, it's probably just a mountain
lion," Dink said. "I hope you don't have
any cookies in your pocket. They can
smell food a mile away!"

Josh laughed. "Nice try, Sly."

They found a few more white tree
markings before they walked out of the

woods into sunshine. In front of them was another pond surrounded by low bushes. This pond was twice as large as the one near the barn. It was also covered with green algae and smelled just as bad.

Ruth Rose walked a little closer to the pond. The ground was soft and muddy. "Guys, people prints," she said. "Just like the ones we saw at the other pond."

Dink noticed some other marks next to the footprints. "These are *tire* marks!" he said.

"But how could a car get back here? There's no road," Josh said.

"We could barely make it through that old trail," Ruth Rose said. "A car never would!"

Dink studied the tracks for a moment. "There are only two tires," he said. "And they're narrow, like a motorcycle's."

"Or a motor scooter, like Hanna's," Ruth Rose added.

"Still, how did it get here?" Dink wondered. He snapped a picture of the marks with his cell phone. "Let's keep looking."

Dink continued walking around the pond, looking for more tire marks. He stopped when he noticed a break in the trees. Small bushes were crushed. Grass was flattened. The spot was ten feet from the edge of the pond. "Guys, over here!" he yelled.

Josh and Ruth Rose ran over.

Dink knelt and snapped another picture. He ran his fingers over the grooves in the dirt. "The same tires made these marks," he said. "Somebody drove *something* here. But why?"

"To find whatever Hanna and Kenny read about in the diary," Ruth Rose said. "But this is all jungle and yucky pond water."

Josh plucked a purple blossom from a vine. "One of these flowers was stuck in Hanna's spokes," he said, handing it to Ruth Rose. "Remember you brought it in the house?"

"Good eye, Josh!" Ruth Rose said. "So Hanna was here, or at least her scooter was!"

They followed the tire marks to the edge of the pond. "That green stuff smells like rotten eggs," Josh said.

"In the magazine Auntie A. lent me, I read that some scientists are trying to turn algae into a new kind of fuel," Dink said.

Josh dipped his rake into the algae. "This slimy stuff?" he asked. Suddenly he jumped back, dragging Dink and Ruth Rose by their arms. "Don't move," he whispered. "There's an alligator in the pond, and he's watching us!"

"Where?" Ruth Rose whispered back.

"Straight ahead," Josh said. "About three feet away from the bank. His shiny eyes are peeking out of the algae!"

Dink looked, shading his eyes with his hand. "Dude, that's floating junk," he said. He used Josh's rake to drag it close enough to grab. What he picked out of the pond was a plastic tube, about six inches long and as big around as his wrist. The tube contained an inch of gooey green algae. It had a red cap and a label with algae covering the words.

"It's just a tube," Dink said. He wiped the label on his shirt. Two lines were printed on it:

3/19/20/T.P.
KENNEDY SPACE CENTER

CHAPTER 12

"Kennedy Space Center?" Ruth Rose said. "What would this be doing here?"

"Good question," Dink said. "The Space Center is like twenty miles away."

The kids explored more of the pond and the woods around its edges. They picked up tin cans, bottles, plastic bags, and an old sneaker. They stuffed it all into one of the bags.

"I think mosquitoes love me," Josh said. He slapped at his neck.

"Me too," Ruth Rose said. She had a red bite on her wrist.

Dink glanced around the pond and the jungle surrounding it. They all had muddy feet and mosquito bites. "Let's go back," he said.

They followed the old trail back to the barn and bunkhouse. "Wait a sec," Dink said. He crossed the yard, glancing toward the picnic table. He didn't see Hanna and Kenny, but her scooter was parked by the back door of the house.

Dink found his pictures of the tire marks and held his phone close to the rear scooter tire. He nodded: the grooves were the same. He ran back to the bunkhouse. "You were right," he told Ruth Rose. "Hanna's scooter made those tire marks we saw!"

"But we still don't know what she and Kenny found there," Ruth Rose said. She left the bag of litter on the ground, and they went inside.

"Check for snakes, you guys," Josh

said. They searched the floor, the bathroom, and the blankets on their beds. No critters.

Dink washed his hands and pulled his laptop from his backpack. He sat on Josh's bunk and booted up the computer.

"What are you doing?" Josh asked.

"Looking to see if there's another way to get to that pond," Dink said.

He found a map of their area. A few seconds later, they were looking at Auntie A.'s house on Palm Lane. Dink widened the map to show a bigger picture. "Check this out!" he said.

The map showed a narrow trail that ran from Palm Lane into the woods. Mostly hidden by trees, the trail wound through jungle toward the back of Auntie A.'s property. "It's another one!" Ruth Rose said.

"A motor scooter could get through there," Josh said.

"Yeah, I know," Dink said. "And I bet

if we followed it, we'd end up back at the pond."

They suddenly heard a car on Auntie A.'s driveway. Ruth Rose looked outside. "It's Walker!" she said.

The kids ran out in time to see Walker stepping out of the car with a leather satchel. The car backed out of the driveway and turned left on Palm Lane. Wallis and Auntie A. came out of the house.

"Why didn't you call us to come and get you?" Wallis asked.

Walker hugged his sister and aunt. "There was an Uber driver waiting at the airport, so I just jumped in," he said.

The kids welcomed Walker, and they all went inside Auntie A.'s kitchen. Walker handed a small wrapped package to his aunt. "Happy birthday, Auntie," he said.

"Thank you, darling!" she said. "I'll open it later with my cake."

Wallis laughed. "Hey! How do you

know there's a cake?" she asked.

Alice just smiled. "Who would like something cold to drink?"

They carried glasses of lemonade outside to the picnic table. Walker told everyone about his time with his friends from the Space Center. This reminded Dink about the tube, and he ran to get it.

"We found it on the other side of the jungle," Josh said as Dink handed the tube to Walker.

"Goodness, what were you doing in there?" Auntie A. asked.

"We were exploring," Ruth Rose said. "Josh saw this floating in the pond. He thought it was an alligator!"

"Do you know what those numbers and letters mean?" Dink asked Walker.

Walker turned the tube in his fingers. "The numbers might be a date from last month," he said.

"Um, we also found tire tracks by the pond," Dink said. He showed everyone the pictures on his phone. "They match the tires on Hanna's scooter."

"What would Hanna be doing way back in that jungle mess?" Auntie A. said.

Walker pointed to Dink's phone. "Mind if I borrow this?" he asked. "My phone's inside."

Dink handed over his phone, and Walker snapped a picture of the tube. "I'll text this to a buddy who works at the Space Center and ask him to show it around." He tapped some buttons and sent the picture on its way.

Alice told her nephew about the mountain lion on the property. "I don't know what I'd have done if the critter hadn't run away," she said. "Good thing Bear was in the house with me!"

Dink's phone rang a few minutes later. He took the call and listened. Then he said, "No, this is Dink Duncan. Walker Wallace sent you the picture on my phone. He's right here."

Dink handed the phone to Walker, who stepped away from the table. They watched him pace with the phone to his ear. After a few minutes, he came back.

"That was Tom Pardue, one of the scientists in the lab," he said. "His initials are on the tube. He and another scientist came here in March to take samples. They didn't realize they'd lost one of their collection tubes."

"Samples of what?" Alice asked.

Walker grinned. "Pond algae," he said. "Tom's really into the stuff. He says a lot of scientists around the world are studying algae because it can be turned into fuel. Algae grows best in hot climates, and your ponds are covered with the stuff."

"But how did Mr. Pardue know about my ponds?" Auntie A. asked. "And I certainly didn't give them permission."

"It's Dr. Pardue, and he said he got a call from a woman claiming to be the owner of this property," Walker said.

"But that's absurd!" Alice said. "I never called him!"

"Not you," Walker said. "Someone *pretending* to be you. She invited Dr. Pardue to come and look at the algae. So they came out and took samples."

"Did they have a motorcycle?" Ruth Rose asked.

"That he didn't mention," Walker said. "But he did say some scientists are researching algae sites in Florida. There's talk of building a facility to study the algae forms that are best suited to make biofuel. Pardue asked the supposed 'owner' if she was interested in selling this property."

"My property is not for sale!" Alice said. She told Walker about the postcards and phone calls urging her to sell.

"Good thing you didn't sell," Walker said. "It's possible that your land is worth a great deal of money to NASA and other industries researching the production of biofuel."

"What's biofuel?" Josh asked.

"A new kind of fuel made from algae

or plants," Walker said. "Most of the fuel we use now comes from fossils, and it's very expensive to get out of the ground. It's also dirty and pollutes the air. Plus, someday there will be no more fossils because we humans will have used them up. So scientists around the planet are spending trillions of dollars to find other ways to make fuel. One of the reasons they're studying algae is because it replaces itself so quickly. And *your* algae is exactly the kind they're looking for, or so Dr. Pardue thinks."

"Do I understand this right?" Wallis asked. "Some woman pretending to own this land called the Space Center and invited scientists to come here?"

"That's what it looks like to me," Walker said. "I guess she got a positive report, because she started pestering Auntie to sell."

He smiled at his aunt. "Hold on to

your land, Auntie. Once we get this figured out, you can sell to NASA if they
want to buy it."

Dink glanced across the table at Josh
and Ruth Rose.

They looked back at him, and Dink
decided it was time to talk. "I think I
know who's trying to cheat you, Auntie
A.," he said.

Three pairs of adult eyes turned to
him.

"Who?" Alice asked.

CHAPTER 13

"Kenny and Hanna," Dink said.

"What!" Wallis cried.

"Explain, please," Auntie A. said.

"Well, you've been getting those post-cards," Dink started. He pulled the latest one from his pocket and laid it on the table. "And calls from someone else wanting to buy your house. You didn't answer them, so I think they're trying a new plan. They're hoping to scare you into leaving."

Dink told them that he thought the snake didn't just wander into the bunkhouse.

"Someone put it there," Ruth Rose said. "They came in while we were asleep and left the snake on the floor."

"I think Kenny or Hanna did it," Dink said. "They know you're afraid of snakes."

Auntie A. smiled. "A lot of people know that," she said. "Why do you think it's Kenny and Hanna?"

"They use a really smelly mosquito repellent, and I smelled it last night in the bunkhouse," Dink said. "I think Hanna wrote the postcards and put them in your mailbox. There was a note from H. on your fridge. I checked the postcard you got yesterday, and the handwriting is the same. I think it's Hanna's. At first, I thought the note might be from Howie because of the H., but—"

"No, only Hanna leaves notes on my fridge," Auntie A. said. "Go on, please."

"Hanna probably called Dr. Pardue," Dink continued. "Kenny is studying botany, so I'll bet he knows that algae can be turned into biofuel. I think Hanna asked Dr. Pardue to come and take samples. He must have told her and Kenny this land could be valuable, so they're trying to get it away from you. Then they'll sell it and make a lot of money!"

"I'll bet they brought Dr. Pardue to the pond on Hanna's motor scooter!" Ruth Rose said.

Alice closed her eyes for a moment. "What about the mountain lion in my driveway?" she asked. "Was that part of the plan to scare me into selling?"

"I don't think there ever was a mountain lion in the driveway," Dink said. "Howie was here, and he didn't see it."

"But I saw the picture on Kenny's phone," Alice said.

"Easy to fake," Josh said. "Wallis, do you have the video of us up in the space simulator?"

Wallis pulled out her phone, found

the video, and pushed the start button. They all looked at the space simulator sailing in the heavens.

"See how it looks like we're traveling through a real sky?" Josh asked. "But the sky isn't real. It's just stars painted on the ceiling and walls. That's sort of how Kenny made it look like there was a mountain lion near your house."

Everyone stared at Josh, waiting.

Josh blushed pink. "I think Kenny took a picture of your driveway," he said. "Then he downloaded a picture of a mountain lion from the internet. He put the two pictures together to make it look like the mountain lion was lying in your driveway, but it wasn't."

"That's right," Dink said. "Your car and Howie's van were both in the driveway yesterday morning. Howie said he washed them before lunch. If Kenny had taken that picture yesterday, the cars would have been in the picture, too. But they weren't, and that means Kenny took the picture some other time."

"Hanna would know how to fake the picture," Ruth Rose said. "She's studying to become a movie producer."

No one spoke for a minute. "So Kenny did that to scare me," Auntie A. said.

"And I wouldn't be surprised if Hanna

lied about seeing a rattlesnake under the picnic table," Ruth Rose said. "For the same reason."

Everyone looked at Auntie A. "All this so they could get me to sell them my property?" she said.

"Which they would sell to the U.S. government for a lot more money," Walker said. "It does look like Kenny and Hanna are trying to scam you, Auntie."

"But they're both just students," Alice said. "They have no money to buy this property."

"But maybe M.K. does," Dink said. He tapped the postcard on the table.

"I'm sorry," Auntie A. said. "Who is M.K.?"

"You were supposed to call M.K. if you wanted to sell," Dink said. "Hanna wrote the postcards and put down the initials and phone number."

"Could M.K. be Hanna or Kenny?" Wallis asked. She opened her phone.

"There's one way to find out." She tapped in the number, put the phone on speaker, and handed it to her aunt. "Let's see who answers."

Everyone heard a man's voice say "Christmas Savings Bank, Mark Keans's office. How may I help you?"

Auntie A.'s eyes grew wide. "Mr. Keans," she said after a few seconds, "this is Alice Wallace speaking. I think you are interested in my property on Palm Lane."

"Why, yes, Ms. Wallace," the man said. "I have a bank customer who loves your property. They are ready to pay all cash, and my bank is prepared to make the loan. Can we sit down together to discuss the details?"

"Say no!" Wallis whispered.

"I have relatives visiting from out of town," Alice said into the phone. "But I'll call you soon to make a date."

Mr. Keans agreed, and the call ended.

"So the mysterious M.K. is Mark

Keans, who works in a bank," Walker said. "But how does he know about this property?"

Auntie A. handed the phone to Wallis. "It's not a mystery," she said. "Kenny's last name is Keans."

CHAPTER 14

"Mark Keans is Kenny's uncle," Dink said. "Kenny told us he was late picking us up yesterday because he had to bring something to his uncle at the bank."

"It all fits together," Ruth Rose said. "Kenny must have told his uncle about how scientists want to turn algae into fuel. They got Dr. Pardue to come out for a look, and then they made a plan to cheat you, Auntie A."

"I can't believe Kenny and Hanna did this," Auntie A. said. "I thought they were my friends. I even invited them for a piece of my birthday cake later!"

"Perfect," Walker said. "We'll have a nice chat with those two!"

Wallis laughed. "I guess I'd better get busy baking!" she said.

The picnic table was crowded when Wallis carried out the cake. Alice had also invited Howie and his wife, Dot, with Seth and Maddy. Bear lay under the table, waiting for cake crumbs.

Hanna and Kenny showed up last, riding on the motor scooter. They parked the bike and quickly sprayed each other with mosquito repellent. Hanna dropped the can in her book bag, and they came across the lawn.

When they reached the table, Dink sniffed the air. It was definitely the same stuff he'd smelled in the bunkhouse last night.

When everyone was seated, Alice said, "Kenny, why don't you call your uncle Mark? Do you think he'd like some of my cake, as well as my property?"

"My uncle?" he said. "How . . . how do you know my uncle?"

Alice tapped the postcard on the table. "We know a lot," she said. "Like how you and Hanna and your uncle tried to get my land from me. How Hanna lied about seeing a rattlesnake under this table yesterday."

"And we know about the mountain lion," Wallis added. "Or should I say fake mountain lion?"

Kenny and Hanna looked at each other. Both had turned red.

Alice placed two slices of cake on a paper plate. "Take these and leave my property," she said. "Enjoy the cake."

"I'll escort you," Walker said. He stood behind Hanna's seat.

"Me too," Howie said, joining Walker.

Dink whispered something to Howie.

"Oh, and we won't report you to the police if you return the diary and Mr.

Wallace's papers," Howie added.

He and Walker followed Kenny and Hanna to the motor scooter. Dink watched Hanna unlock the small compartment and pull out a thin book and a file folder. She handed them to Walker, then climbed onto her scooter with Kenny on the rear seat. They left their slices of cake on the driveway and sped away.

. . .

After Howie and his family had gone, Dink, Josh, Ruth Rose, and Wallis sat at the picnic table. They could hear Walker and Alice laughing through the kitchen window.

"My aunt wanted me to tell you that you can visit her whenever you want," Wallis said. "And she'll bake you cookies forever."

"Awesome," Josh said. "But I ate too much cake, and my stomach hurts."

Ruth Rose giggled. "Now you know why *you* are the Red Gobbler!" she said.

Dink gazed up at the moon. "I see Blinky," he said.

"Oh, I'd forgotten about Blinky with all the other excitement," Wallis said. "He's still up there!"

"I figured out a way to bring him back to Earth," Dink said.

"Tell me!" Wallis said.

"What if there was a podcast for people who own cats?" Dink said. "You could call it *CatChat.* In your story, the astronaut who lost Blinky could ask all the cat owners to send one dollar each to NASA. It would get millions of dollars and use the money to send Blinky's owner to the moon. He'd get Blinky and bring him back home!"

Josh started laughing. *"CatChat?"* he said.

"Well, I like the idea," Ruth Rose said. "It would be a happy ending!"

"I think it's brilliant!" Wallis said. "I'm going to work that into the story. I'll put a note in the book telling my readers how Dink Duncan came up with the idea."

"Dinky saves Blinky," Josh said. He gave Dink a poke.

Ruth Rose rolled her eyes.

Dink grinned.

DID YOU FIND THE
SECRET MESSAGE
HIDDEN IN THIS BOOK?

If you *don't* want
to know the answer,
don't look at the bottom
of this page!

GET THE FACTS FROM A TO Z!

To learn more about the facts in this mystery, find these books at your local library or bookstore:

Books About the International Space Station

The International Space Station by Allan Morey (Epic, 2018)

Life in Space by Ben Richmond (Sterling, 2018)

My Journey to the Stars by Scott Kelly (Crown, 2017)

Books About Astronaut Training

Almost Astronauts: 13 Women Who Dared to Dream by Tanya Lee Stone (Candlewick, 2009)

Ask the Astronaut: A Galaxy of Astonishing Answers to Your Questions on Spaceflight by Tom Jones (Smithsonian, 2016)

Astronaut in Training by Kathryn Clay (Capstone, 2017)

Books About Animal Tracks

Go Wild: Be a Tracker by Chris Oxlade (Hungry Tomato, 2015)

Tracks Count: A Guide to Counting Animal Prints by Steve Engel (Craigmore Creations, 2014)

Books About Snakes

Awesome Snake Science! by Cindy Blobaum (Chicago Review, 2012)

Copperheads by Melanie A. Howard (Capstone, 2012)

Rattlesnakes by Heather L. Montgomery (Capstone, 2011)

Snakes by Valerie Bodden (Creative Company, 2009)

Books About Big Cats

Crazy About Cats by Owen Davey (Flying Eye, 2017)

Florida Panthers by William Caper (Bearport, 2007)

Mountain Lions by Christine Zuchora-Walske (Capstone, 2012)

Pumas by Charlotte Guillain (Raintree, 2014)

Books About Algae and Biofuel

Protists: Algae, Amoebas, Plankton, and Other Protists by Rona Arato (Crabtree, 2010)

Renewable Energy: Discover the Fuel of the Future by Joshua Sneideman and Erin Twamley (Nomad, 2016)